T0199006

The Basset Hound Pitbull Mixed Named BEETHOVEN

DUSTIN REIS

To order additional copies of this book, contact:
Xlibris
1-888-795-4274
www.Xlibris.com
Orders@Xlibris.com

ISBN: Softcover   978-1-9845-8020-7
       EBook   978-1-9845-8019-1

Print information available on the last page

Rev. date: 05/20/2020

The Basset Hound
Pitbull Mixed Named
BEETHOVEN

DUSTIN REIS

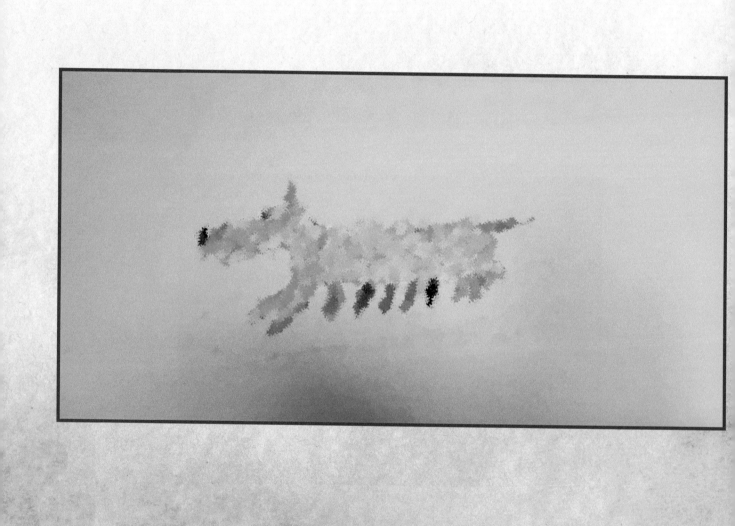

Once upon a time on a cold December night were born seven Basset Hound Pitbull Mix puppies. They were all so cute but only one stood out the most. His name was Beethoven.

Beethoven had blue eyes and his whole body was mixed with tan and white. He had cute white legs.

As days had passed, it was time to find new homes for Beethoven and his siblings. One day people came from all over to pick up their puppy, but for Beethoven, he had to be dropped off to his new home.

When the time came for Beethoven to meet his new owner, it was the most exciting day for both him and his owner named Bob.

For the first time, Beethoven also met his new best friends, Woody, an Old English Sheepdog and Foxy, a Schnauzer and Westie Mix.

That same day Beethoven was all cozy on a blue rounded rug. He was so cute that even Bob and his friends thought it was adorable.

One day Beethoven's brother, Boomer came over to visit. Beethoven and Boomer were so excited to see each other.

On the same day, they were so excited, that they started to play tug of war with each other.

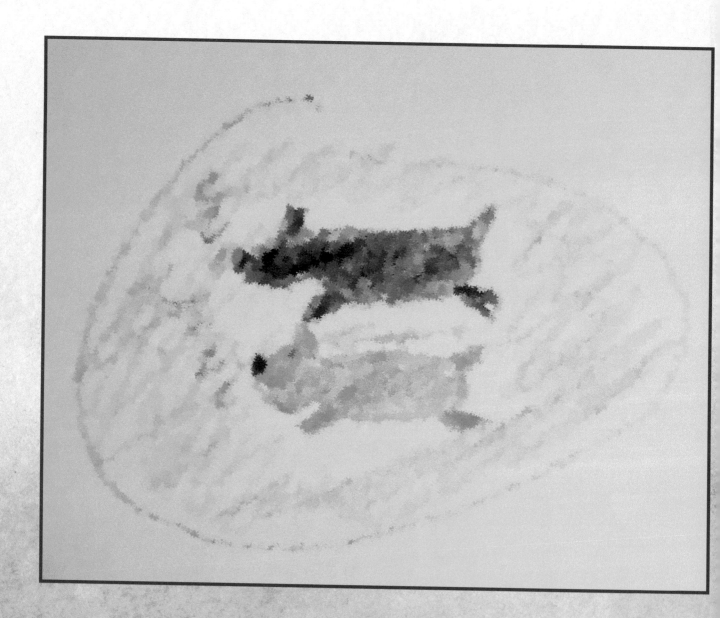

As night came, the two were sleeping side by side and on top of each other.

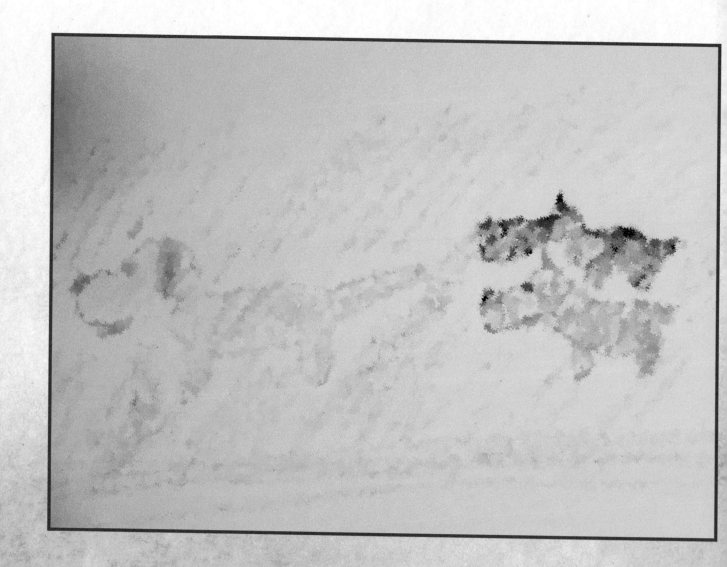

The next day, the brothers were
playing around in the kitchen,
and chasing Foxy's tail.

One day Beethoven and Foxy were on the Patio all covered with snow. They started to play for a while.

Months came to pass, and Beethoven was getting big. His eyes were now brown. He weighed 30lbs.

One sunny day, Bob started to train Beethoven to walk on a leash and go potty outside. He also started to train Beethoven to sit and come. But Beethoven did not want to listen.

Instead, Beethoven wanted to play with toys and other dogs. So, Bob decided that he would join in with the fun and play fetch with Beethoven. Bob and Beethoven enjoyed the day of fun and they both lived happily ever after.

About the Author

Dustin Reis is a Full-time Student at Iowa State University, currently living in Ames, Iowa. In his free time, Dustin loves playing the piano, going to church, being around his friends and family. But also loves spending time with his dog Beethoven.

About Beethoven

Beethoven is an 8-month-old Basset Hound Pitbull mix, who loves to play and go for walks. He loves to have his belly rubbed every day and be around other people.

Printed in the United States
By Bookmasters